JASON

QUEST FOR THE GOLDEN FLEECE

A
GREEK
MYTH

STORY BY
JEFF LIMKE

PENCILS BY
TIM SEELEY

INKS BY
BARBARA SCHULZ

BASED ON
THE HEROIC POEM
BY APOLLONIUS
OF RHODES

EUROPE

ITALY

MEDITERRANEAN SEA

JASON

QUEST FOR THE GOLDEN FLEECE

COLCHIS

BLACK SEA

BITHYNIA

A GREEK MYTH

GREECE

HELLESPONT

THESSALY

AEGEAN SEA

IOLCUS

ATHENS

GRAPHIC UNIVERSE™ • MINNEAPOLIS

The legend of Jason and the other Greek heroes aboard the *Argo* and their quest for the Golden Fleece may have originated as a story told about the first great sailing ships built by the ancient Greeks. The legend as it is told today was first written in about 280 b.c. by Apollonius of Rhodes, a librarian at the great library in Alexandria, Egypt. The author also based this version on the retellings in *Bulfinch's Mythology*, *Mythology* by Edith Hamilton, and *The Friendly Guide to Mythology* by Nancy Hathaway. David Mulroy of the University of Wisconsin–Milwaukee ensured historical and visual accuracy.

STORY BY JEFF LIMKE

PENCILS BY TIM SEELEY

INKS BY BARBARA SCHULZ

COLORING BY HI-FI DESIGN

LETTERING BY RAY DILLON

**CONSULTANT: DAVID MULROY,
UNIVERSITY OF WISCONSIN–MILWAUKEE**

Copyright © 2007 by Lerner Publishing Group, Inc.

Graphic Universe™ is a trademark of Lerner Publishing Group, Inc.

Graphic Universe™
An imprint of Lerner Publishing Group, Inc.
241 First Avenue North
Minneapolis, MN 55401 U.S.A.

Website address: www.lernerbooks.com

Library of Congress Cataloging-in-Publication Data

Limke, Jeff.

TABLE OF CONTENTS

THE CLASHING ROCKS

MY NAME IS JASON, AND I SHOULD BE THE RULER OF IOLCUS.

MY FATHER, AESON, HAD THE THRONE TAKEN AWAY FROM HIM BY HIS BROTHER PELIAS. MY FATHER HID ME FROM THE EVIL PELIAS, AND I WAS RAISED BY A CENTAUR, HALF MAN, HALF HORSE, NAMED CHIRON. CHIRON TAUGHT ME WELL WHO I WAS AND WHAT I WAS SUPPOSED TO BE.

WHEN I ARRIVED IN IOLCUS TO CLAIM MY BIRTHRIGHT, MY UNCLE DIDN'T GIVE THE THRONE TO ME. HE SAID HE WOULD ACCEPT MY CLAIM TO THE THRONE ONLY IF I BROUGHT HIM THE FLEECE OF THE GOLDEN RAM OF COLCHIS.

HE SAID BRINGING THE GOLDEN FLEECE TO IOLCUS WOULD GRANT HIM PEACE FROM THE GHOST OF PHRIXUS, WHO HAUNTED HIM NIGHTLY. AND THE ADVENTURE WOULD BRING TO ME GREAT GLORY.

I BUILT A GREAT SHIP AND NAMED IT THE ARGO, AND I GATHERED ALL THE HEROES I COULD FIND TO JOIN ME ON IT.

THE HEROES INCLUDED NOBLE AND VIRTUOUS PELEUS WHO WAS GIVEN A SEA GODDESS TO WED, AND ZETES AND CALAIS THE SONS OF BOREAS, THE NORTH WIND.

WE ARGONAUTS TRAVELED FAR ON OUR SEARCH AND HAD MANY ADVENTURES.

BLIND PHINEUS, WHOM THE HEROES SAVED FROM STARVATION, RODE WITH US AS WELL.

OTHERS, SUCH AS HERCULES, HAD LEFT US EARLIER.

THE TWINS, CASTOR AND POLLUX, BROUGHT THEIR YOUTHFUL ENERGY, WHILE ORPHEUS BROUGHT HIS LYRE TO KEEP US ENTERTAINED.

HERCULES HAD SAVED HIS ARMOR-BEARER HYLAS FROM DROWNING AND HAD STAYED BEHIND TO MAKE SURE HE RETURNED TO GOOD HEALTH.

THEN A NEW DANGER PUT OUR VERY LIVES AT RISK.

JASON, I CAN TELL FROM THE SOUNDS THAT WE ARE NEAR THE ROCKS KNOWN AS THE SYMPLEGADES. I TOLD YOU ABOUT THEM. NO SHIP HAS EVER PASSED THROUGH THEM SAFELY.

9

ORPHEUS PLAYED HIS LYRE ON INTO THE NIGHT. HIS TALES OF WONDER AND HEROISM, ENHANCED BY HIS MELODIOUS VOICE, CAPTIVATED US ALL.

THE GODS HAD SUPPORTED US THUS FAR. I BELIEVED THEY WOULD CONTINUE TO DO SO AS LONG AS WE REMEMBERED TO HONOR THEM.

IN HONOR OF ZEUS, GOD OF THE SKY AND THUNDERBOLTS; HERA, HIS WIFE AND GODDESS OF THE HOME; AND POSEIDON, GOD OF THE WATERS WE SAILED UPON—

I GIVE THIS PART OF OUR CELEBRATION IN THANKS AND INVITE THEM TO JOIN US—

—AND ASK THEM TO TAKE US QUICKLY TO COLCHIS, HOME OF THE GOLDEN FLEECE.

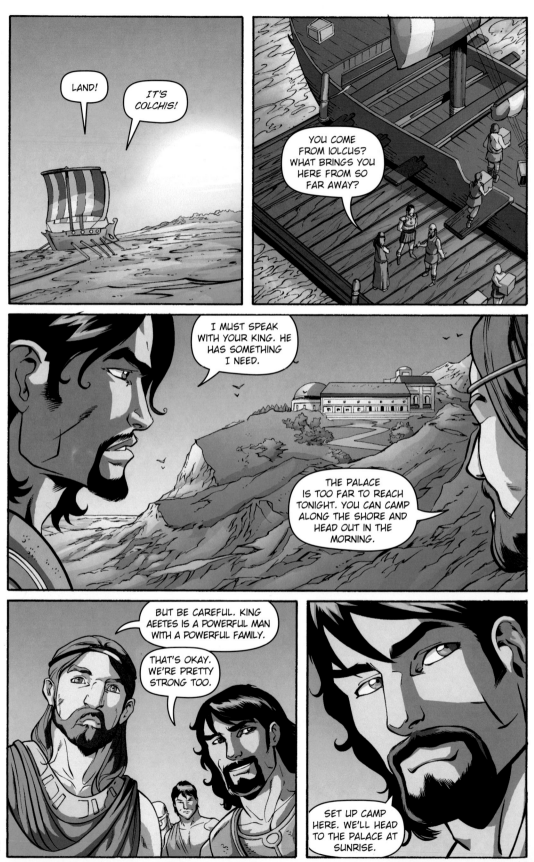

SHE TOLD HIM HE WOULD HAVE TO SACRIFICE HIS CHILDREN BY NEPHELE TO ZEUS AND HERA.

NEPHELE PRAYED TO THE GODS TO PROTECT HER AND HER CHILDREN.

IT LOOKED AS THOUGH THE GODS HAD IGNORED HER.

NEPHELE TRIED TO SAVE HER CHILDREN. SHE BEGGED FOR THEIR LIVES AS THE GUARDS RESTRAINED HER.

THE BOY, PHRIXUS, AND THE GIRL, HELLE, GIGGLED AS THEY LOOKED UP AT THEIR FATHER. THEY THOUGHT HE WAS PLAYING SOME SORT OF GAME.

THEY WERE WRONG. DISTRAUGHT, NEPHELE CALLED OUT ONCE MORE TO THE GODS TO SAVE HER CHILDREN.

THE GODS HAD HEARD HER.

ZEUS SENT A GOLDEN RAM TO SAVE THE CHILDREN.

THE RAM FLEW OFF TOWARD A PLACE WHERE THE CHILDREN WOULD BE SAFE.

HELLE BECAME SO EXCITED, SHE LOST HER GRIP AND FELL INTO THE SEA BELOW. THE GODS CALLED THE PLACE WHERE SHE LANDED THE HELLESPONT IN HER HONOR.

THE RAM FINALLY LANDED HERE IN COLCHIS.

KING AEETES AND PHRIXUS SHEARED THE RAM OF ITS GOLDEN FLEECE BEFORE PHRIXUS OFFERED THE ANIMAL TO ZEUS IN THANKS FOR HIS SAFE ARRIVAL.

PHRIXUS THEN MARRIED AEETES' SISTER CHALCIOPE, AND THEY HAD FIVE CHILDREN TOGETHER.

WHEN I RETURN WITH THE FLEECE, PELIAS WILL HAVE NO CHOICE BUT TO ACCEPT MY RIGHT TO RULE IOLCUS.

15

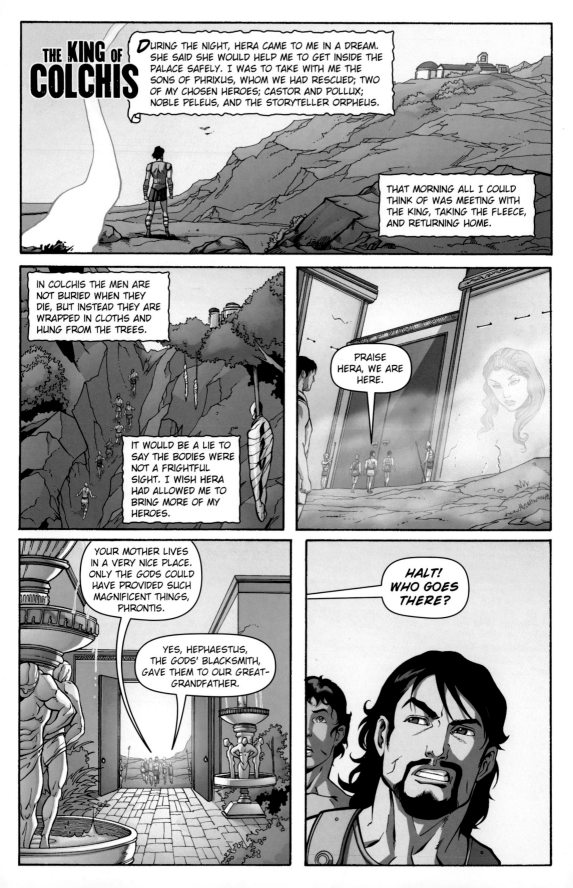

THE BOYS' SHIP HAD RUN AGROUND AFTER THE HELMSMAN WAS STRUCK BY A FEATHER.

FLYING ABOVE THEM WERE THE TERRIBLE BIRDS FROM THE ISLAND OF ARES.

THE BIRDS DEFEND THEMSELVES BY LOOSENING FEATHERS FROM THEIR BODIES AND LETTING THEM DROP.

THE POINT OF THE QUILL IS AS SHARP AS A SPEAR AND JUST AS DEADLY.

MELAS! *THERE! DO YOU SEE IT?*

IT'S AN ILLUSION OFF THE WATER, PHRONTIS.

NO, LOOK CLOSER—

MELAS! THEY SEE IT TOO!

HERE! HERE!

LOOK HERE!

A FIRE! WE NEED A FIRE!

PRAY TO HERA AND ZEUS THAT THEY SEE IT.

PRAY TO POSEIDON TO LET THEM COME THIS WAY.

22

23

25

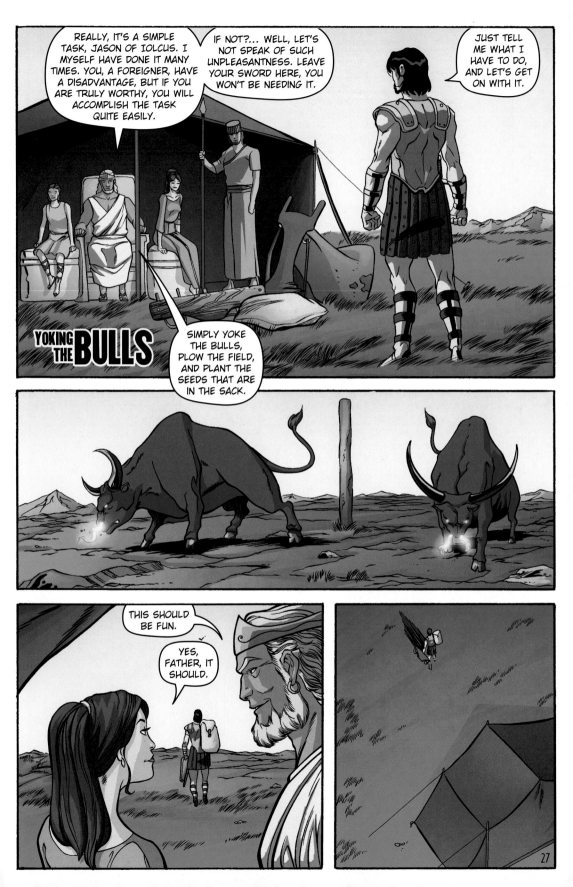

YOKING THE BULLS

GROWING UP WITH A CENTAUR AS MY TEACHER, I LEARNED MANY THINGS THAT MOST ROYAL CHILDREN WOULD HAVE MISSED.

MOST PRINCES ARE WELL TRAINED TO BE SOLDIERS. I WAS TOO.

BUT MOST AREN'T TRAINED IN HOW TO CAPTURE FARM ANIMALS.

I WAS.

BUT I HAVE TO ADMIT THAT THIS WAS A BIT DIFFERENT THAN TENDING SHEEP AND GOATS ON A MOUNTAINSIDE.

YAH! BULL!

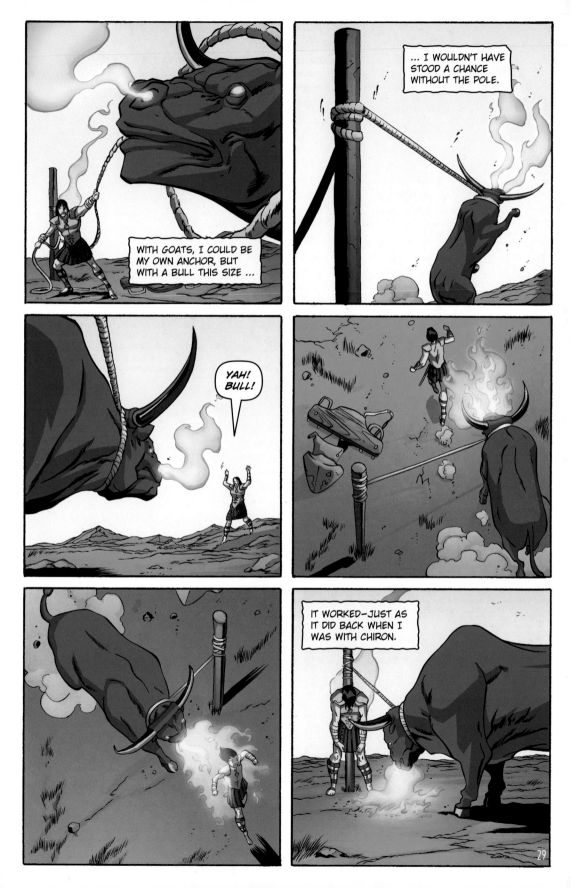

THE SECOND BULL WAS AS EASY TO YOKE AS THE FIRST. WITH MEDEA'S OINTMENT, THE FLAMES TICKLED RATHER THAN BURNED. WITHOUT THAT OINTMENT, I WOULD HAVE BEEN NOTHING MORE THAN A CHARRED BODY.

THE BULLS ARE YOKED, KING AEETES.

IS THIS THE FIELD I'M TO PLOW AND SEED?

YOU WERE RIGHT, MEDEA. HE WAS GREAT.

I'VE NEVER SEEN ANYONE ELSE YOKE THE BULLS ALONE BEFORE.

QUIET. THAT IS NOT HOW A PRINCE SHOULD SPEAK. IF HE SUCCEEDS, HE COULD TAKE THIS KINGDOM AS HIS OWN, AND THEN WHAT WOULD YOU HAVE?

YES, FATHER. I UNDERSTAND.

HAVING PLOWED AND SEEDED BEFORE, I KNEW WHAT TO EXPECT, NOT LIKE YOKING THOSE BULLS.

THAT HAD SCARED ME, BUT WITH MEDEA'S OINTMENT, IT WENT WELL.

SOWING THE FIELDS

ALL I HAD TO DO WAS TAKE A HANDFUL OF SEEDS AND SPRINKLE THEM INTO THE FURROW LEFT BY THE PLOW.

THIS WAS TOO EASY.

THE SEEDS WERE BIG. BIGGER THAN ANY I KNEW ABOUT.

WHAT IS THIS?

WHAT KIND OF SEEDS ARE THESE?

WHAT ARE THESE? WHAT DO THEY GROW?

THEY ARE DRAGON'S TEETH. BUT YOU'LL HAVE TO WAIT AND SEE WHAT WE HARVEST.

31

OUTSIDE THE CAVE, NIGHT HAD FALLEN AND AEETES HAD NODDED OFF.

ARGONAUTS! TO THE SHIP!

THE FLEECE! MEDEA! ABSYRTUS!

STOP THEM AT ALL COSTS!

GET THE FLEECE!

THEY'VE KIDNAPPED THE PRINCE AND PRINCESS!

41

HEE-EE-ELP ME-EE!

SAVE HIM!

ROPE! THROW HIM A ROPE!

GOT YOU, BOY. YOU'RE SAFE. YOU MUST WORSHIP POSEIDON.

AND IF YOU DON'T, NOW WOULD BE A GOOD TIME TO START.

CAREFUL!

43

HE'S SAFE.

I KNEW HE WOULD BE. MY FATHER WOULD NEVER LET ANYTHING HAPPEN TO HIM.

YOU WERE THAT SURE?

IT TURNED OUT THE RIGHT WAY, DIDN'T IT? DOES IT MATTER WHETHER I WAS SURE OR NOT?

AND NOW WE RETURN TO IOLCUS?

YES, THAT'S THE PLAN. I'VE GOT THE FLEECE. THE QUEST IS DONE, AND I WILL BECOME KING.

AND I WILL BE QUEEN.

OF COURSE. I PROMISED YOU I WOULD NEVER FORGET YOU.

NEVER?

NEVER.

AND I'LL ALWAYS LOVE YOU.

GLOSSARY AND PRONUNCIATION GUIDE

ABSYRTUS (ab-*sir*-tus): prince of Colchis

AEETES (ee-*ee*-teez): king of Colchis

AESON (*eeh*-sun): father of Jason; king of Iolcus

ARGO (*ar*-goh): Jason's ship

ARGONAUTS (*ar*-goh-nawtz): the heroes who sailed with Jason

ATHAMAS (ah-*tham*-as): a king of Iolcus

ATHENA (*uh*-thee-nuh): goddess of wisdom and war

BOREAS (*bor*-ay-us): the North Wind

CADMUS (*kad*-mus): founder of the Greek city of Thebes who planted the dragon teeth that grew into warriors

CALAIS (kal-*ay*-us): one of the twin sons of Boreas

CASTOR (*kas*-tor): one of the Greek hero twins

CHALCIOPE (kal-*kee*-oh-pee): Aeetes' daughter; wife of Phrixus

CHIRON (*keer*-un): the centaur (part horse, part man) who raised Jason

EROS (*eh*-rohs): god of love

HELLE (*hel*-lee): princess of Argos; daughter of Athamas and Nephele

HEPHAESTUS (heh-*fes*-tus): the blacksmith god

HERA (*hehr*-uh): wife of Zeus and goddess of the home

INO (*ee*-no): Athamas's second wife

JASON: hero who traveled to Colchis to retrieve the Golden Fleece

MEDEA (muh-*dee*-uh): princess of Colchis

MELAS (*may*-las): son of Phrixus and Chalciope

NEPHELE (*neh*-feh-lay): cast-off queen of Iolcus

ORPHEUS (*or*-fee-us): Greek hero and musician

PELEUS (*pay*-lay-us): famous hero; future father of Achilles

PELIAS (*pay*-lee-us): brother of Aeson; stole the throne of Iolcus

PHINEUS (*fin*-ee-us): a wise man

PHRIXUS (*frik*-sus): prince of Iolcus who was taken to Colchis by the Golden Ram

PHRONTIS (*fron*-tis): son of Phrixus and Chalciope

POLLUX (*pohl*-ux): one of the Greek hero twins

POSEIDON (po-*sy*-dun): god of the oceans and of earthquakes

SYMPLEGADES (simp-*leg*-uh-deez): massive rocks in the sea that crash together when ships try to pass

ZETES (*zay*-teez): one of the twin sons of Boreas

ZEUS (*zoos*): chief Greek god; the god of thunder and of the sky

FURTHER READING AND WEBSITE

Day, Nancy. *Your Travel Guide to Ancient Greece*. Minneapolis: Twenty-First Century Books, 2001. Day gives advice to tourists traveling back to ancient Greece, including places to visit, food to try, what to wear, and how to get around.

Hamilton, Edith, *Mythology*. Boston: Little, Brown, 1942. Hamilton's classical book retells the stories of Greek gods and heroes, as well as Roman and Norse myths.

Mythweb. http://www.mythweb.com/index.html. This site, with a searchable encyclopedia, provides readers with information on gods, goddesses, and places in Greek myth.

Riordan, James. *Jason and the Golden Fleece*. London: Frances Lincoln, 2005. This is a modern retelling of the adventures of Jason and the Argonauts in a picture-book format.

Zarabouka, Sofia. *Jason and the Golden Fleece: The Most Adventurous and Exciting Expedition of All the Ages*. Los Angeles: Getty Publications, 2004. This is an exciting and dramatic retelling of the legend with hauntingly eerie illustrations.

CREATING *JASON: QUEST FOR THE GOLDEN FLEECE*

The legend of Jason and the other Greek heroes aboard the *Argo* and their quest for the Golden Fleece may have originated as a story told about the first great sailing ships built by the ancient Greeks. The legend as it is told today was first written in about 280 B.C. by Apollonius of Rhodes, a librarian at the great library in Alexandria, Egypt. The author also based this version on the retellings in *Bulfinch's Mythology*, *Mythology* by Edith Hamilton, and *The Friendly Guide to Mythology* by Nancy Hathaway. David Mulroy of the University of Wisconsin-Milwaukee ensured historical and visual accuracy.

original pencil sketch from page 27

INDEX

ABOUT THE AUTHOR AND THE ARTIST

JEFF LIMKE was born and raised in North Dakota where he never braved an ocean adventure, fought skeletons, or stole a golden fleece. Jeff's books for the Graphic Myths and Legends series include *King Arthur: Excalibur Unsheathed*; *Isis & Osiris: To the Ends of the Earth*; and *Thor & Loki: In the Land of Giants*. He has published other stories with Caliber Comics, Arrow Comics, and Kenzer and Company.

TIM SEELEY is a professional comic book artist and writer. Hailing from the backwoods of central Wisconsin, Seeley currently resides in Chicago, Illinois, where he works as staff artist for Devil's Due Publishing. His resumé includes *G.I. Joe*, *Forgotten Realms*, and *Hack/Slash*. He thanks the ancient Greeks for having a story with zombies in it.